ALI BABA AND THE FORTY THIEVES, one of the best known of the famous *Arabian Nights* tales, is adapted here by Anne Terry White. All children will enjoy reading about how Ali Baba overhears some thieves opening the door of a wealth-filled cave with magic words. He tells his brother Kasim about the cave, but Kasim is found in the cave by the robbers and is killed. Then the robbers plot to kill Ali Baba, but his slave Morgiana uses chalk, oil, and her cleverness to outwit the robbers and defeat their plot.

ABU KIR AND ABU SIR, a lesser known tale from the *Arabian Nights,* involves a dyer and a barber who decide to travel about and share the wealth they will make from their crafts. Abu Kir proves to be a selfish man, for when he becomes wealthy, he does not share his good fortune with Abu Sir. But Abu Sir is kind and pardons his comrade even when he learns that Abu Kir tried to have him killed.

Richly retold in the Arabian tradition, the tales in this book are part of the new "Myths, Tales, Legends" grouping of Garrard's Reading Shelf.

Ali BaBa
Abu Kir
and
Abu Sir

TWO ARABIAN TALES
ADAPTED BY ANNE TERRY WHITE

ILLUSTRATED BY PAUL FRAME

GARRARD PUBLISHING COMPANY
CHAMPAIGN, ILLINOIS

Contents

ALI BABA and the FORTY THIEVES

ABU KIR and ABU SIR

Ali Baba and the Forty Thieves

1. "Open, O Sesame!"

A long time ago, in a certain town of Persia, there lived two brothers. One was named Kasim and the other Ali Baba. When their father died, they divided between them the little he left them and lost no time in wasting and spending it all. However, the elder brother, Kasim, soon married the daughter of a rich merchant. Thus when the merchant died, Kasim became the owner of a large shop filled with rare goods and a storehouse stocked with costly stuffs. He also had much gold that was buried in the ground. Thus he was known throughout the city as a rich man.

But the woman Ali Baba married was as poor as himself. They lived, therefore, in a mean hut, and Ali Baba earned a bare living by selling firewood. Every day he collected it in the forest and carried it to market upon his three donkeys.

One day Ali Baba had cut enough dead branches and dry wood for his need and had loaded the wood on his three donkeys. Suddenly he saw a cloud of dust rising in the air. It was moving rapidly toward him. He looked sharply and saw a troop of horsemen about to reach him.

This sight greatly alarmed Ali Baba. They may be bandits, he thought, who will slay me and drive off my donkeys.

In his fright, he began to run. But as the men were near and he could not escape out of the forest, he drove his animals loaded with wood into some bushes. Then he climbed into a huge tree that grew close beside a high rock. There he sat down on a branch from which he could see everything beneath him, while none below could see him.

The horsemen—all young, strong riders—came close up to the rock and dismounted. Ali Baba counted them —they were forty in number. From their looks and manner he decided that they were indeed bandits. Clearly these men had robbed a caravan and had brought their booty to this place to hide it.

As soon as the robbers came under the tree, each of them unbridled his horse and tied it. Then each took off his saddlebags. One man, who seemed to be the captain, took his load on his shoulder and pushed forward with it through thorns and thickets. When he came to a certain spot, he spoke these strange words: "Open, O Sesame!"

At once a wide doorway appeared in the face of the rock. The robbers went in. Last of all, their chief followed. Then the door shut of itself.

They stayed in the cave a long time. Meantime Ali Baba was forced to sit in the tree, fearing to move. If he

6

climbed down, he thought, the bandits might at that very moment come out and seize and slay him. At last he decided to mount one of the horses, and driving his donkeys before him, return to town.

He was about to do this when suddenly the door flew open. The robber chief was the first to come out. Standing at the entrance, he counted his men as they passed out. Then he spoke the magic words: "Shut, O Sesame!"

At this the door again closed. Each man then slung his saddlebags on his horse and mounted. Then they all rode off in the direction from which they had come.

Ali Baba stayed up in the tree watching them. Nor would he come down until they were gone clean out of sight.

When he climbed down, he thought to himself, I too will try those magic words and see if at my bidding the door will open and close.

So he called out aloud, "Open, O Sesame!"

No sooner had he spoken than the door flew open. He went in and saw a large cave, high as a tall man. It was hewn out of the living rock. Light came in through air holes in the rock which formed the roof.

Ali Baba had expected to find nothing but gloom in this robbers' den. He was amazed. From floor to ceiling the cave was heaped with bales of silk and brocade and embroidered cloth and mounds on mounds of carpeting.

8

Besides this he saw gold and silver coins without measure, piled on the ground and in leather bags and sacks.

Thieves must have stored their gains in this place for years and years, thought Ali Baba.

When he had entered the cave, its door had closed behind him. But he was not frightened because he had kept in his mind the magic words.

"Open, O Sesame!" he commanded, and the door opened again.

He paid no attention to the precious stuffs around him, but began at once to carry out the sacks of coin. When he had taken out as much as his donkeys could carry, he loaded the animals. He covered the sacks with branches so that none might see the bags and people would think he was carrying home his usual ware. Lastly he called out, "Shut, O Sesame!" And the door closed.

For the spell worked like this: When anyone *entered* the cave, the door shut of itself behind him; when he *came out* of the cave, the door did not close again till he had pronounced the words, "Shut, O Sesame!"

2. Kasim Learns the Secret

Ali Baba urged his donkeys on as fast as he could. When he got home, he drove the animals into the court-yard. Then shutting the outer door tight, he unloaded the wood and carried the bags of gold in to his wife. She felt them. Finding them full of coins, she began to scold Ali Baba, for she thought he had turned robber.

"Indeed, I am no robber," he said. "Rejoice with me at our good fortune."

And he told her of his adventure and began to pour the gold from the bags in heaps before her. She was dazzled by the glitter and was delighted with the story of his adventures. Then she started counting the coins.

"O silly woman," said Ali Baba. "How long will you continue turning over the coins? Now let me go dig a hole to hide this treasure, so that none may know its secret."

"Right you are!" said she. "Still, I would like to weigh the money and have some idea of its amount."

"As you please, but tell no one about it," he replied.

So she went off in haste to Kasim's home to borrow weights and scales. She could not find Kasim, so she spoke to his wife, saying, "Lend me, I pray you, your scales for a moment."

"Do you need the bigger scale or the smaller?" asked Kasim's wife.

"I do not need the big scales. Give me the small ones," the other answered.

Kasim's wife said, "Stay here a moment while I look about and find what you want."

With this she went into another room. There she took the scales and secretly smeared fat and wax over the pan of the balance that she might know what thing Ali Baba's wife would weigh.

For, she thought to herself, some bit of it will stick to the fat and the wax.

Ali Baba's wife didn't suspect anything. She carried home the scales and began to weigh the gold. Meantime her husband did not stop digging. When the money was weighed, the two put it in the hole and carefully covered it with earth. Then the good wife took the scales back, not knowing that a coin had stuck to the pan.

When Kasim's wife saw the gold coin, she fumed with envy and wrath.

So ho! she said to herself. They borrowed my scales to weigh out gold?

She marveled greatly where so poor a man as Ali Baba had got such wealth, and that evening when Kasim returned home, she said to him, "O man, you think yourself rich. But lo, your brother Ali Baba is a nobleman beside you and far richer than you are. He has such heaps of gold that he must weigh his money with scales, while you are satisfied to count your coin."

"How do you know this?" asked Kasim.

Then she told him all about the scales and showed him the gold coin, which bore the mark and name of some ancient king.

Kasim had no sleep that night because of his envy. Next morning he got up early and went to Ali Baba.

"O my brother," he said, "you appear to be poor and needy. But in fact you have such wealth that you must weigh your gold with scales."

"What are you talking about!" said Ali Baba. "I do not understand you."

Kasim flew into a rage.

"Don't pretend!" he cried. "And don't think to deceive me!" And he showed Ali Baba the gold coin, saying it had stuck to the pan of the scales. "You have thousands of gold coins such as these!" he ended.

Then Ali Baba saw that the matter could not be hidden. So he told his brother everything about the bandits and the treasure in the cave.

When he had heard the story, Kasim said, "Tell me where the place is. Also the magic words by which the door opened and closed. And I warn you, if you do not tell me the whole truth, I will let the Judge know about your coins. Then all your wealth will be taken from you, and you will be disgraced and thrown into jail."

12

So Ali Baba told him all. Kasim listened carefully to everything and next day set out, driving ten mules that he had hired. And he found the rock and the tree where Ali Baba had hidden himself.

"Open, O Sesame!" he cried in great joy.

The door opened wide at once. Kasim went in and saw the piles of jewels and treasures all around. And as he stood among them, the door shut after him.

He walked around marveling at the treasures. When he got tired of this, he gathered together enough bags of gold coin to load the ten mules and placed the bags by the entrance, ready to be carried out. But he had clean forgotten the magic words!

He cried out, "Open, O Barley!"

The door did not move.

Kasim named all kinds of grains, but not sesame. That word had slipped from his mind as though he had never heard it. In his distress he now paid no heed to the gold that lay heaped by the door. He paced to and fro, backward and forward. And the sight of the gold that a short time ago had filled him with such joy and gladness now caused him grief and sadness.

It happened that at noonday the robbers came by that way. From afar they saw some mules standing beside the entrance to the cave and marveled how the beasts had wandered so far. For Kasim had not tied them, and they were browsing here and there in the forest.

As the robbers had done before, they dismounted when they came to the rock. The captain again repeated the magic words and at once the door flew open.

Kasim had heard the horses drawing near and nearer. At first he fell to the ground in terror, for he was sure that these were the robbers and that they would slay him. Then he took courage. The moment the door flew open, he rushed out, hoping to escape. But the unhappy man ran full into the captain, who felled him to the ground. One of the band at once drew his sword and with one blow cut Kasim in two.

Then the robbers rushed into the cave. They saw the bags of gold Kasim had heaped by the door, ready to take away. They put the bags quickly back again, but they did not miss what Ali Baba had taken. However, they wondered greatly how the man they had killed had got in. The rock was high and steep. They knew it was not possible for anyone to climb in through the skylights, and none could enter by the door unless he knew the magic words that would open it.

After some thought, they cut Kasim's body into four parts and hung them on the inside of the door as a warning to anyone who dared enter the cave. Then they went out, the captain ordered the door to close, and the band rode away.

3. A Dead Man Gets Sick and Is Made Whole

Now when night fell and Kasim did not come home, his wife became uneasy in her mind. She came running to Ali Baba and said, "O my brother, Kasim has not returned. You know where he went, and I am sore afraid some misfortune has happened to him."

Ali Baba also feared there had been some mishap. But he tried to comfort his sister-in-law with words of cheer. He said: "O wife of my brother, Kasim is just being cautious. He is avoiding the city and coming by a roundabout road. This is the reason he has not come. He will be here soon."

Kasim's wife went home comforted and sat waiting for her husband's return. But when half the night was spent and still Kasim did not come, she was like one gone mad. She feared to cry aloud lest the neighbors should learn her secret. So she wept in silence.

Why did I tell Kasim the secret, she thought, and make him envy Ali Baba? This is what has come of it — this terrible trouble has fallen upon me.

She spent the rest of the night in bitter tears, and in the morning she went in hottest haste to Ali Baba.

"O my brother," she said, "I pray you, go and look for Kasim!"

Ali Baba tried to comfort her, and at once set out with his donkeys for the forest. When he reached the rock, he saw fresh stains of blood. And not finding his brother or the ten mules, he felt some evil was in store. Then he went to the door and saying, "Open, O Sesame!" he went in.

There was the dead body of Kasim, two parts hanging to the right and two to the left of the entrance. Ali Baba was terrified. Quickly he wrapped the quarters in two cloths and laid them upon one of his donkeys. Then he carefully hid the cloths with sticks, that none might see them. On the two other animals he placed bags of gold and covered them most carefully, too. And when all was done, he closed the cave door with the magic words and set off home.

When he got home, Ali Baba turned the donkeys bearing the coins over to his wife and bade her bury the gold at once. But he did not tell her about the condition in which he found Kasim. He went with the third beast to his brother's house and knocked gently on the courtyard door.

Now Kasim had a slave girl, clever and sharp-witted, Morgiana by name. She softly drew back the bolt and let Ali Baba and the donkey into the courtyard of the house. Then Ali Baba took the body from the beast's back and said: "O Morgiana, make haste to perform the burial rites for your master. I will go tell the

17

news to your mistress and will quickly return to help you in this matter."

At that instant Kasim's widow saw her brother-in-law and cried: "O Ali Baba, what news do you bring me? Alas, I see grief written on your face! Say quickly what has happened!"

Then he told her what had happened and in what way he had brought home the dead body. "We must keep this matter secret," he added, "because our very lives depend on it."

The widow wept with sore weeping and made answer, "I give you my word to keep the affair hidden."

Then Ali Baba went to Morgiana. He told her the whole story of the robbers. They talked together a long time about how to manage the burial of his brother. Then, with many warnings, he left the slave girl and went home, driving his donkey before him.

As soon as Ali Baba was gone, Morgiana went quickly to a druggist's shop. There she asked for a drug often given to very sick people.

"Who is there in your house that lies so ill as to require this medicine?" the druggist asked as he gave it to her.

"My master Kasim," she said. "He is sick almost unto death. For many days he has not spoken, nor tasted a bit of food, so that we almost despair of his life. I pray the medicine will help."

Next day Morgiana went again and asked the druggist for more medicine, such as is given to one who is at the door of death. The man gave it to her and she took it, and sighed aloud, and wept, saying: "I fear me he will not have strength to drink this. I think all will be over with him before I return to the house."

Meanwhile Ali Baba was anxiously waiting to hear sound of wailing from Kasim's house that he might go and join in the funeral rites.

Early on the second day, Morgiana veiled her face and went to the shop of an old tailor, Baba Mustafa by name, who made shrouds for the dead. As soon as she saw him open his shop, she put a gold piece in his hand and said, "Bind a bandage over your eyes and come along with me."

But Baba Mastafa held back. At this Morgiana put a second gold coin in his hand and begged him to go with her. The tailor then consented. When they had gone some way, Morgiana tied a kerchief tightly over his eyes. Then she led him by the hand to the house where lay her master's dead body. Taking off the bandage in the darkened room, she bade the tailor sew together the quarters of the body. After this she threw a cloth upon the body and said, "Now make haste and sew a shroud for this dead man and I will give you yet another gold piece."

Baba Mustafa quickly made a shroud to fit, and

Morgiana paid him. Then once more bandaging his eyes, she led him back to the place from which she had brought him blindfolded. There she left him and returned home. Then with the help of Ali Baba she got the body ready for burial.

This done, Morgiana went to the mosque. There she gave notice that her master had died and brought back a man with her to read the prayers for the dead. After the prayers, the coffin was carried off on the shoulders of four neighbors. And Morgiana walked before it with bare head, striking her breast and weeping and wailing, while Ali Baba and the rest of the neighbors came behind.

In such order they entered the cemetery and buried Kasim. After this all went their ways. The women of the quarter, according to the custom of the city, came and sat an hour with Kasim's widow, comforting her and leaving her somewhat cheered. And Ali Baba stayed forty days at home to mourn for his brother.

Thus nobody in the town knew the secret except Ali Baba, Kasim's widow, and Morgiana. When the forty days of mourning were ended, Ali Baba moved all his property and his family to Kasim's house. And he put his brother's eldest son, who understood trade, in charge of the shop to carry on the dead man's business.

4. Chalk Marks on the Door

In time it chanced that the robbers went again to the treasure cave. They marveled greatly to find no sign or trace of Kasim's body. They saw, also, that much gold had been carried off.

"Now we must inquire into this matter," the captain said. "Else we shall suffer great loss. Our treasure, which we and our forefathers have collected over many years, will little by little be stolen away."

All could see that the man they had slain was not the only one who knew the magic words, since someone had come and carried off the body and also much gold. It was clear that they must find this man, whoever he might be.

The robbers talked it over and decided that one of them must go to the city disguised as a foreign merchant. There he must go from quarter to quarter and street to street and learn if any townsman had lately died, and if so, where the man had lived.

At this one of the robbers said: "Grant me leave to go and find out such things in the town and bring you word. And if I fail, take my life."

So the bandit disguised himself and went at night into the town. Next morning early he went to the market square. He saw that the only shop open was that of Baba Mustafa the tailor. Thread and needle in hand, he sat upon his work stool. The thief bade him good day and said: "It is yet dark. How can you see to sew?"

"I see that you are a stranger," the tailor replied. "Though I am old, my eyesight is keen. Only yesterday I sewed together a dead body while sitting in a room quite darkened."

"You are jesting with me," the bandit said. "You mean you sewed a shroud for a dead body."

The tailor answered: "It does not matter to you. Ask me no more questions."

At this the robber placed a gold coin in the tailor's hand, saying, "I do not desire to discover anything which you hide. This only would I learn from you: in what house did you do that job? Can you direct me there or lead me there yourself?"

The tailor took the gold with greed and answered, "I have not seen with my own eyes the way to that house. A certain slave woman led me to a place which I know right well, and there she bandaged my eyes. She guided me to some house and then took me into a darkened room. There she unbound the kerchief, and showing me the dead body cut in pieces, bade me first sew together the body and then make the shroud. Afterward she again blindfolded me and led me back to the place from which she had brought me. So you see that I am not able to tell you where to find the house."

Said the robber: "Although you do not know the house, still you can take me to the place where you were blindfolded. Then I will bind a kerchief over your eyes, and you lead me as you were led. Perhaps in this way you may hit upon the house. If you will do this favor for me — see, here is another gold piece for you." And the bandit slipped a second gold piece into the tailor's palm.

Baba Mustafa put it into his pocket with the first. Then, leaving his shop as it was, he walked to the place where Morgiana had tied the kerchief around his eyes.

There the robber bound on the bandage and led the tailor by the hand.

Baba Mustafa, who was clever and keen-witted, soon struck the street by which he had gone with the woman. He walked on, counting step by step. Then suddenly he halted.

"Thus far I came with her," he said.

The two had stopped in front of Kasim's house, where his brother Ali Baba now lived. The robber then made marks with white chalk upon the door so that he might readily find it at some future time.

Removing the bandage from the tailor's eyes, he said: "O Baba Mustafa, I thank you for this favor. Allah reward you for your goodness! Tell me now, I pray you, who lives in that house?"

"In truth, I know not," the tailor said. "This is a quarter of the city that I do not know well."

The bandit understood that he could get no further clue from him. So with many thanks he let the tailor go to his shop, while he himself hurried to the place in the forest were the band was waiting for him.

Not long afterward, it so happened that Morgiana went out upon some errand. She marveled greatly when she saw the chalk marks showing white on the door. She stood a while deep in thought. She guessed at once that some enemy had made the signs that he might recognize the house and do some harm to her lord. She therefore

chalked the doors of all her neighbors in the same manner. And she kept the matter secret, telling neither her
master nor her mistress.

Meanwhile the robber told his comrades his tale of
adventure and how he had found the house. So the
captain and all the band went to the city by different
ways. And he who had placed the mark on Ali Baba's
door went with his chief to point out the place. He took
him straight to the house and showed him the sign.

"Here," said he, "lives the man we are in search of."

But when the captain looked around him, he saw
that all the houses bore chalk marks after the same
fashion. And he said, "How do you know which house of
all these houses that bear the same signs is the one of
which you speak?"

The robber guide was greatly confused. At first he
could make no answer. Then with an oath he cried: "I
did indeed set a sign upon a door, but I do not know
where all the other marks came from. Nor can I surely
say which is the door I chalked."

At that the captain returned to the market place,
where his men were waiting, and said to them: "We have
toiled in vain. We have not found the house we went out
to seek. Let us return now to the forest."

5. The Captain Turns Oil Merchant

They trooped off. And when the robbers had all met in the treasure cave, the captain imprisoned the man who had led them to the city for nothing. And he said, "I will show special favor to anyone who will go into town and bring me news whereby I may lay hands on the thief who has taken our property."

At this, another of the company came forward and said: "I am ready to go and inquire into this. I will bring you what you desire."

The captain gave him presents and promises and sent him to the city. By chance this second robber went first to the house of Baba Mustafa the tailor just as the thief before him had done. In the same way he persuaded the tailor with gifts of golden coin. And in like manner he was guided to Ali Baba's door. Here he put a mark with red chalk on the door jamb. Then he stole back to his company and boasted: "O our captain, I have found the house and put a mark on it. I will distinguish it clearly from its neighbors."

But, just as before, Morgiana marked all the doors in the same fashion, and kept the matter secret. So when the troop came there, they saw each and every house in the neighborhood marked with signs of red chalk. So they again returned disappointed. And the captain, growing very angry, imprisoned the second spy also.

Then the chief said to himself: Two men have failed and have met with just punishment. Now I myself will go and find the house of this fellow.

Baba Mustafa, who had gained many gold pieces in this matter, led the captain to the house of Ali Baba. But the chief made no chalk sign, only marking the house on the page of his memory. Then he returned to the forest.

"I know the place now," he said to his men. "There will be no difficulty in finding it. Go straight off and buy me nineteen mules. And buy and bring also one large leather jar of mustard oil and seven-and-thirty empty jars of the same kind. Without me and the two who are in jail, there are thirty-seven of you. I will stow you away, armed, each in his jar. I will load two jars upon each mule. And on the nineteenth mule there shall be a man in a jar on one side, and the other jar will be full of mustard oil.

"I, for my part, will disguise myself as an oil merchant and drive the mules into town. Arriving at the house by night, I will ask its master to let me stay in his yard till morning. During the dark hours we shall rise up and fall upon him and slay him. And when we have made an end of him, we will take the gold and treasure he has robbed us of and bring it back upon the mules."

The plan pleased the robbers. They went forth and bought the mules and the huge leather jars. After a delay of three days, shortly before nightfall, they arose. Each hid himself inside an empty jar. The chief then put on the dress of a trader and placed the jars on the nineteen mules. This done, he drove the beasts before him and reached Ali Baba's place at nightfall.

It chanced that Ali Baba was strolling to and fro in front of his home after supper. The captain made him a low bow and said: "I come from a distant village with oil. I have often been here to sell oil. But to my grief I have arrived in town too late and do not know where to spend the night. I pray you, let me stay here in your courtyard and ease the mules by taking down the jars and giving the beasts some fodder."

Now when Ali Baba was up in the tree, he had heard the captain's voice and had seen him enter the cave. But because of the disguise, he did not recognize the leader of the thieves. With hearty welcome he said yes, the trader could halt there for the night. Then he pointed out an empty shed where the mules could be tied and bade one of the slave boys bring them grain and water.

He also gave orders to Morgiana, saying: "A guest has come here and will stay the night. Busy yourself with all speed about his supper and make the guest bed ready for him. He will be coming in very soon."

When the captain had let down all the jars and had fed and watered his mules, Ali Baba received him with all courtesy and kindness. Then he called Morgiana and said to her: "See that you do every service for this stranger of ours. See that he lacks nothing. And tomorrow I wish to go to the Baths. So give my slave boy Abdullah a suit of clean white clothes which I may put on after bathing. And make some broth overnight that I may drink it on my return home."

"I will have all in readiness," Morgiana replied.

Ali Baba retired to his rest. The captain, after eating his supper, went to the shed and saw that all the mules had food and drink for the night. And as he walked about, he whispered to his men who were in ambush, "At midnight when you hear my voice, quickly slit the leather jars open with your knives from top to bottom and come out without delay."

After this he went to his chamber, Morgiana showing him the way with a lamp.

"If you need anything more," she said, "I pray you, command me, who am ever ready to obey your word."

"I need nothing more," he answered. Then putting out the light, he lay down on the bed to sleep a while till the time came to rouse the men and finish off the work.

6. Boiling Oil

Meanwhile Morgiana did as her master had bidden her. First she took out a suit of clean white clothes and gave it to Abdullah, who had not yet gone to rest. Then she placed the pot on the hearth to boil the broth and blew up the fire till it burned briskly. After a short delay she wanted to see if the broth was boiling. But by that time all the lamps had gone out, and the oil was all gone.

The slave boy Abdullah saw she was troubled and said to her: "Why make such a to-do? There are many jars of oil in the shed. Go and take as much as you like."

Morgiana thanked him for his idea and went out, while Abdullah, who was lying at his ease in the hall, went off to sleep.

With the oil can in her hand, the slave girl walked to the shed where stood the leather jars, all ranged in rows. Now, as she drew near one of them, the thief who was hidden there heard the tread of footsteps. He thought it was his captain, for whose call he was long waiting. So he whispered, "Is it time now for us to come out?"

Morgiana started back in fright at the sound of a human voice. But as she was bold and ready of wit, she replied softly, "The time has not yet come."

To herself she said: These jars are not full of oil. There is some kind of mystery here. The oil merchant is hatching some plot against my master. Allah protect us from his snares!

Then she went to the next jar, and when the man inside spoke, she made her voice like the captain's and gave the same reply. And so on to the jars one by one, all but the last.

Then she said to herself: Praise the Lord! My master took this fellow in, believing him to be an oil merchant. But lo! He has let in a band of robbers who only await the signal to fall upon him and kill him.

Then she passed on to the last jar. Finding it full of oil, she filled her can and returned to the kitchen. There she trimmed the lamp and lit the wick. Then she set a huge pot on the fire, filled it with oil from the jar, heaped wood on the hearth, and fanned the fire to a fierce flame. When the oil boiled, she bailed out a potful at a time and carried it to the shed, where she poured it into the leather jars one by one. So all the thieves, being unable to get out, were scalded to death. Noiselessly, so that no one in the house knew anything about it, the slave girl made an end of them all.

Now when she had made sure that every one of the men had been slain, she went back to the kitchen. She shut the door and sat watching the kettle of broth.

An hour passed before the captain awoke from

sleep. Opening his window, he saw that all was dark and silent. So he clapped his hands as a signal for the men to come out. But not a sound was heard in return. After a while he clapped again and called aloud, but got no answer. When he cried out a third time and got no reply, he didn't know what to make of it.

Perhaps they have all fallen asleep, he thought to himself. The time for action has come. I will have to wake them up at once. And he went to the shed where the jars stood.

Coming to the nearest jar, he was startled by the smell of hot oil. Touching the outside of the jar, he felt it hot. Then going to the others one by one, he found all in the same condition. Then he knew what fate had overtaken his band. Fearing for his own safety, he climbed the wall and made his escape.

Morgiana waited a while to see if the captain returned from the shed. But he did not. She knew then that he had climbed the wall and fled, for the street door was double-locked. The thieves being all taken care of, Morgiana lay down to sleep with an easy mind.

7. "Beware the Captain, Who Fled from Here Alive!"

The sun was high when Ali Baba returned from the Baths. He marveled greatly to see the jars still standing under the shed. He said to Morgiana, "How comes it that the oil merchant my guest has not taken his mules and jars of oil to the market?"

Morgiana answered: "May Allah keep you safe! I will tell you in private about this merchant."

So Ali Baba went with the slave girl. First she locked the courtyard door. Then pointing to a jar, she said, "I pray you, look in and see if there is oil there or something else."

So Ali Baba peered inside and saw a man. He cried aloud at the sight and would have fled in his fright. But Morgiana said: "Fear him not. This man can no longer do you harm — he lies dead and stone dead."

Hearing her words, Ali Baba asked: "O Morgiana, what evils have we escaped? And by what means has this wretch met death?"

She answered him: "Praise be to Almighty Allah! I will tell you all about it. But hush! Do not speak loud lest the neighbors learn the secret and it end in trouble for us. Look now into all the jars, one by one, from the first one to the last."

So Ali Baba looked into one jar after another, and in each jar he found a man fully armed lying scalded to death. At first he was speechless from amazement. Then he asked, "And where is he, the oil merchant?"

"I will tell you about him, too," she answered. "The villain was no trader, but one who would have brought death upon you. Now, I will tell you what he was and what has happened. But you are fresh from the Baths. Go in! You should first drink some of the broth for your health's sake."

So Ali Baba went inside, and Morgiana served up the broth. When he had drunk it, he said, "I pray you, tell me this wondrous story and set my heart at ease."

At this, Morgiana told him the whole story from first to last.

"O master," she said, "when you retired to rest and bade me boil the broth, your slave did your command. I took out a suit of clean white clothes and gave it to the boy Abdullah. Then I kindled the fire and set on the broth. As soon as it was ready, I needed the lamp so that I might see to skim it. But all the oil was gone. When I learned this, I told Abdullah, and he advised me to draw some oil from the jars which stood under the shed. So I took a can and went to the first jar.

"Suddenly I heard a voice inside whisper cautiously, 'Is it time to come out?'

"I guessed at once that the pretended merchant had laid some plot to slay you. So I replied, 'The time has not yet come.'

"Then I went to the second jar and heard another voice. I made the same answer, and so on with all of them. I was sure now that these men were only waiting for some signal from their chief, this pretended merchant whom you took in as a guest. I realized he had brought these men to murder you and plunder your goods. But I gave him no chance to do it.

"I found that the last jar was full of oil. So I took

some and lit the lamp with it. Then putting a large kettle on the fire, I filled it up with oil from the jar and made a fierce blaze under it. When the oil was boiling hot, I took out a potful at a time, and going to each jar, I poured boiling oil into it. In this way I destroyed all the robbers. Then I returned to the kitchen, put out the lamp and stood by the window watching what would happen next.

"Not long after, the robber captain awoke and signaled to his thieves. Getting no reply, he came downstairs, went out to the jars, and finding that all his men were slain, he fled through the darkness, I know not where. Then with my heart at rest, I slept."

Thus spoke Morgiana, and then she added: "I have told you the whole truth. For some days I suspected something, but I kept it from you, fearing it might get to the neighbors' ears. But now I will tell you about it.

"One day as I came to the door of the house, I spied a white chalk mark on it. A few days later I saw a red sign beside the white. I did not know what the marks were made for. Nevertheless I put the same kind of marks on the doors of some of the neighbors, thinking that some enemy had done this deed, intending to do my master harm. That way, I thought, it would be hard to know house from house.

"Judge now and see if these signs and all this villainy are not the work of the bandits of the forest, who marked our house that they might recognize it. Of these forty thieves there are yet two left of whom I know nothing. So beware of them. But chiefly beware the captain, who fled from here alive. Take good heed and be cautious, for if you fall into his hands, he will not spare you but will surely murder you. And I will do all that lies in my power to save my lord and his property from hurt."

Hearing these words, Ali Baba rejoiced and said: "I am well pleased with you for the way you behaved. Tell me what you would have me do for you. I shall never forget your brave deed as long as there is breath in me."

But Morgiana said, "What we have to do is bury these bodies in the ground so the secret should not be known to anyone."

At this Ali Baba took the slave boy Abdullah into the garden. There under a tree they dug a deep pit and dragged the bodies to it and threw them in. Then covering up the remains of the seven-and-thirty robbers, they made the ground level and clean as it had been. They also hid the leather jars and the arms. And soon Ali Baba sent the mules by ones and twos to the market and sold them all with the able help of Abdullah.

Thus the matter was hushed up. It did not reach the ears of anyone. However, Ali Baba continued to be ill at ease, fearing that the captain and the other two robbers would work him harm.

8. The Robber Captain Plots Again

Meanwhile, after escaping with his life, the captain of the thieves rushed angrily to the forest. He was all confused and the color had fled from his face. He thought the matter over and over again. At last he firmly resolved that he must take the life of Ali Baba. If he did not, he was sure that he would lose all his treasure. His enemy knew the magic words and could come into the cave at will. What is more, he determined to do everything alone. After he got rid of Ali Baba, he would get together another band of thieves and they would go on doing what his ancestors had done for generations.

So he lay down to rest that night, and rising early in the morning, he went to the city and stopped at the first inn he came to.

Doubtless, he thought, the murder of so many men has reached the Judge's ears. Ali Baba must have been seized and his house torn down and his goods taken away. And the people must surely have heard about it.

So he went at once to the keeper of the inn and asked, "What strange things have happened in the city during the last few days?"

The innkeeper told him all that he had seen and heard. But the captain could not learn a thing about what he wanted to know. Then he understood that Ali Baba was very wary and wise and had got away not only with the treasure but with the murders also.

I must have all my wits about me, the captain said to himself. If not, I will fall into his hands and perish.

With this in mind, he hired a shop in the market place. Here he brought whole bales of the finest stuffs from the cave. And he took his seat in the store and began to trade, calling himself Hasan.

By chance his place was just across the way from Kasim's shop, where his son, Ali Baba's nephew, now traded. The captain took pains to become friends with all the shopkeepers around. But he was most friendly to the son of Kasim, who was a handsome and well-dressed youth. Often the captain would chat with him.

Soon after the robber hired the shop, it chanced that Ali Baba came to see his nephew, as he often did. The captain saw and recognized him at once. And a few days later he asked the young man, "I pray, tell me, who is he that comes now and again to your shop?"

"He is my uncle, the brother of my father," the youth answered.

At this the captain showed the young man even more favor. He gave him presents, invited him to eat with him, and fed him with the daintiest of dishes.

After a time Ali Baba's nephew thought it was only right and proper that he should invite the merchant to supper. But as his own house was small and he could not show much splendor, he took counsel with his uncle. And Ali Baba said to his nephew, "You are right. You should entertain your friend in the same fashion as he entertained you. Tomorrow is Friday and you will be shutting your shop as all good merchants do on that day. After the early meal, take Hasan for a walk to smell fresh air. And as you walk, lead him here. Meanwhile I will give orders to Morgiana to make ready the best of food for a feast. Do not trouble yourself in any way — just leave the whole thing in my hands."

So next day Ali Baba's nephew took Hasan to walk about the gardens. As they were returning, he led him by the street where his uncle lived. When they came to the house, the youth stopped at the door, knocked on it, and said: "O my lord, this is my second home. My uncle has heard much about you and your goodness to me. He desires greatly to see you. So if you would consent to enter and visit him, I shall be truly glad and thankful to you."

Just then the door was opened by the porter. Ali Baba's nephew seized his companion's hand and eagerly led him in.

The master of the house received him with all possible courtesy.

"O my lord," Ali Baba said to Hasan, "I am much obliged and thankful to you for showing favor to the son of my brother. I see that you are even fonder of him than I am."

Hasan replied with pleasant words and said: "Your nephew has greatly taken my fancy. For although he is young in years, Allah has given him much wisdom. I like to sit and chat with him."

Thus they talked, and after a time the guest rose to depart. Ali Baba, however, would not let him leave.

"Where are you going, O my friend?" he said. "I pray you, sit at meat with us and after that go home in peace. Perhaps the dishes are not as delicate as those you are used to, but do stay and refresh yourself with my food."

Hasan replied: "O lord, I thank you for your kind invitation, and I would sit at meat with you with much pleasure. But for a special reason I have to excuse myself. By order of the doctor who lately cured me of a sickness I must not eat any food prepared with salt."

Now he said this because one may not eat salt with someone whom he intends to kill. But Ali Baba did not guess his reason.

"If this be all," he said, "do not deprive me of the honor of your company. As the meats are not yet cooked, I will forbid the cook to make use of any salt. Stay here a while and I will return."

9. Dance of Death

So saying, Ali Baba went in to Morgiana and bade her not to put salt into any of the dishes.

"Who is this man who eats meat without any salt?" she asked.

"What does it matter to you who he may be?" Ali Baba answered. "Just do my bidding."

"It is well," she said. "All shall be as you wish."

But in her mind Morgiana wondered at the man who made such a strange request and desired to look at him. So when all the meats were ready for serving up, she helped the slaveboy Abdullah to spread the table and set on the meat. No sooner did she see Hasan than she knew who he was. Moreover, she looked at him closely and spied a dagger under his robe.

So ho! she thought to herself. This is the reason why the villain eats no salt. He seeks an opportunity to slay my master, whose enemy he is. However, I'll get ahead of him. He shall not harm my lord.

When all had eaten their fill, Abdullah brought Morgiana word to serve the dessert. So she cleared the table and set on fresh fruit and dried fruit. Then she placed a little table by the side of Ali Baba with three cups and with a flagon of wine. And lastly she went off

47

with Abdullah into another room, as though she would eat supper herself.

Then the captain of the robbers, seeing that the coast was clear, said to himself: The time has come. With one thrust of my dagger I will finish off this fellow and escape across the garden. If his nephew so much as moves a finger or toe, another stab will settle him. Still, I must wait until the slave boy and the cook maid shall have eaten and lain down to rest in the kitchen.

Morgiana, however, was watching him closely from the other room. She read what was in his mind and she thought, By some means I must stop him and at once put an end to his life.

So the trusty girl changed her dress in all haste and put on such clothes as dancers wear. She veiled her face with a costly kerchief. Around her head she bound a fine turban. About her middle she tied a waist-cloth worked with gold and silver, and into this she stuck a dagger.

Then she said to Abdullah, "Take your tambourine that we may sing and dance in order to entertain our master's guest."

So he got the tambourine and the two went into the room, the boy playing and the girl following. Then bowing low, they asked leave to perform and make sport and play.

"Dance now," said Ali Baba, "and do your best that our guest may be merry."

And Hasan said, "O my lord, you do indeed provide much pleasant entertainment."

Then Abdullah began to strike the tambourine while Morgiana rose up and pleased them with her graceful dancing. Suddenly she drew her dagger from her belt and brandished it as she paced from side to side. And this pleased them most of all. At times also she stood before them, now clapping the sharp-edged dagger under her armpit, now setting it against her breast.

Lastly she took the tambourine from the slave boy Abdullah. Still holding the dagger in her right hand, she went around to ask for coins, as is the custom among entertainers.

First she stood before Ali Baba, who threw a gold coin into the tambourine. His nephew likewise put in a gold piece. Hasan, seeing her about to approach him, began to pull out his purse. Then Morgiana took courage and quick as lightning plunged the dagger into his heart, and the villain fell back stone dead.

10. Morgiana's Reward

"O unhappy girl!" Ali Baba cried out. "What is this deed you have done to bring about my ruin!"

But she replied: "Nay, O my lord! Rather to save you and not to cause you harm have I slain this man. Loosen his garments and see what you will discover under them!"

So Ali Baba searched the dead man's dress and found a dagger hidden there.

Then Morgiana said: "This wretch was your deadly enemy. Look at him well! He is none other than the oil merchant, the captain of the band of robbers. It is because he came here with intent to take your life that he would not eat your salt. When you told me he wished no salt in the meat, I suspected him, and as soon as I saw him I was sure he meant to kill you. Almighty Allah be praised that it is even as I thought."

Then Ali Baba said, "Lo, twice you have saved me from his hand!" And embracing Morgiana, he cried, "As a reward for your loyalty, I set you free, and you shall be my nephew's wife."

Then turning to the young man, he said: "Do as I bid you and you shall prosper. I would have you marry Morgiana, who is a model of virtue and loyalty. You see now that Hasan was your friend only that he might find

a chance to take my life. But this maiden with her good sense and her wisdom has slain him and saved us."

Ali Baba's nephew at once consented. Then the three bore the body out and buried it in the garden.

In due time Ali Baba married his brother's son to Morgiana. All the neighbors came to the wedding and made merry with singing and dancing.

For fear of the thieves, Ali Baba had not once visited the treasure cave since the day he brought home the body of his brother Kasim. But some time after the wedding he mounted his horse and went there. Finding no signs of man or horse, he drew near the door. Then dismounting from his beast, he tied it to a tree, and going to the entrance, pronounced the words which he had not forgotten: "Open, O Sesame!"

At once the door flew open. He entered. There lay the goods and the gold and silver almost as he had left them. So he felt sure that not one of all the thieves remained alive and that he was the only soul who knew the secret of the place.

He took a load of gold coins as great as his horse could carry and brought them home. And in after days he showed the treasure cave to his sons and his sons' sons and taught them how the door could be caused to open and shut. Thus Ali Baba and his household lived all their lives in wealth and enjoyment in the city where he had been a poor woodcutter.

Abu Kir and Abu Sir

1. "Let Us Go to Other Lands"

In the city of Alexandria there once lived two men. One was a dyer named Abu Kir, and the other a barber, Abu Sir. They were neighbors in the market street, where their shops stood side by side.

Now the dyer was a very good dyer, but he was a liar and a cheat, a very bad man. Nor was he ashamed of any shameful thing he did. When anyone brought him cloth for dyeing, he would first demand money to buy dye. So the customer would give him his pay in advance. The dyer would then spend all he got on food and drink. After this he would sell the cloth itself, as soon as its owner turned his back, and waste the money in eating and drinking, always of the very best. And when the owner of the cloth came to him, he would say, "Come back tomorrow before sunrise and you will find your stuff dyed."

The customer would go away and return next day. Then the dyer would say to him: "Come tomorrow. Yesterday I was not at work because I had guests and was attending to their wants all day. But come tomorrow before sunrise and you will find your cloth dyed."

So the customer would go away and come back on the third day, when Abu Kir would say to him: "My wife had a baby in the night, and all day I had many things to attend to. But come tomorrow without fail and take your cloth dyed."

When the man came again, he would put him off with some other excuse. Finally the customer would lose patience and demand: "How often will you say to me 'Tomorrow'? Give me my stuff: I will not have it dyed."

Then the dyer would answer, "By Allah, O my brother, I am ashamed to tell you the truth."

"Tell me what happened!" the other would exclaim.

And Abu Kir would reply: "I dyed your stuff just beautifully and hung it on the drying rope. But it was stolen and I don't know who stole it."

If the owner of the stuff was a kindly man, he would say, "Allah will make it up to me." If he was ill-natured, he would threaten and insult Abu Kir. But whatever the customer did, he would get nothing out of Abu Kir, not even if he went and made a complaint to the Judge.

Abu Kir went on like this till people took to warning one another about him. They all kept away from him. Only those who didn't know the kind of man he was came to him. And his trade grew slack.

He used to go and sit in the shop of his neighbor Abu Sir the barber, facing his dye shop and keeping his eyes on the door. Whenever he saw anyone who didn't know him at the dye-shop door, he would go up and say, "What do you want?"

The man would show him a piece of cloth and reply, "Take this thing and dye it for me."

"What color will you have it?" Abu Kir would ask. And when the man had told him, he would say, "Give me my wage in advance and come tomorrow and take the stuff."

The stranger would advance him the money and go away. Then Abu Kir would carry the cloth to the market street and sell it and buy meat and vegetables and tobacco and fruit and whatever else he needed. But whenever he saw at the door of his shop anyone who had given him stuff to dye, he would not come out. He wouldn't show himself.

In this way he lived for years and years. Then one day he received some cloth from a man with a very bad temper. Abu Kir sold the cloth and spent the money. The owner came looking for him every day but didn't find him, for Abu Kir had fled into the shop of the barber. At last that angry man, getting tired of this treatment, went to the Judge. The Judge sent one of his sergeants to the shop. He nailed up the door, sealed it, took the key, and said to the neighbors: "Tell him to bring back this man's cloth. When he has done that, he can come to me and get his key."

Then the barber said to Abu Kir: "What kind of bad business is this? Whoever brings you something, you go and lose it for him. What has become of this angry man's stuff?"

"O my neighbor," replied Abu Kir, "it was stolen from me."

"That is extraordinary!" said Abu Sir. "Whenever anyone gives you anything, a thief steals it from you! Is your shop the meeting place of all the rogues in town? But I think you are lying. Now tell me the truth."

Then Abu Kir said, "O my neighbor, nobody has stolen anything from me."

"What then do you do with the people's property?" Abu Sir asked.

The dyer answered, "I sell it and spend the money."

"Is this permitted you by Allah?" Abu Sir asked in amazement.

Abu Kir answered, "I do it because business is slack with me and I am poor and have nothing."

Then he went on to complain about how bad things were for him and how little he had.

Abu Sir had troubles of his own. He, too, made very little profit from his business.

"I am master of my craft," he said. "There isn't my equal in this city. But no one comes to me to have his hair cut because I am poor and my shop is in a poor and miserable quarter."

Then Abu Kir said: "O my brother, why should we remain in this town? Let us depart from it, you and I. Let us go to other lands, carrying our crafts in our hands. Dyeing and barbering are in demand the world over. We shall breathe fresh air and rest from our troubles."

Abu Kir didn't stop talking about traveling till the barber began to want to set out too. So they agreed on a route and agreed to travel together.

Then Abu Kir said to Abu Sir: "O my neighbor, we have become brothers and there is no difference between us. He who gets work shall feed him who is out of work. Whatever is left, we will put in a chest. And when we return to Alexandria, we will divide it fairly and equally."

"So be it," replied Abu Sir.

To seal their bond, they repeated the Opening Chapter of the Koran, their holy book. Then Abu Sir locked up his shop and gave the key to its owner. As for Abu Kir, he let his key remain with the Judge's sergeant. The very next day they took their baggage and embarked upon the salt sea.

2. On the Sea

The ship they sailed in carried a hundred and twenty men besides captain and crew. To Abu Sir's great good luck, there was not a barber on the vessel besides himself. So when they loosed the sails, he said to the dyer: "O my brother, this is the sea, and we shall need meat and drink. This voyage will be long and we have very little provision. I think I will take my bowl and razor and towel and go around among the passengers. Maybe someone will say to me, 'Come here, O barber, and shave me.' And I will shave him for a hunk of bread, or a silver piece, or a draft of water. So we shall profit by this, I and you too."

"There is no harm in that," replied the dyer. And he laid his head down and went to sleep while the barber took his things and, going among the passengers, shaved this one and that one. Each man he shaved gave him bread or cheese or water or olives, or even coins.

Among the rest, Abu Sir shaved the captain. While the barber was at it, he talked about his lack of food for the voyage. And the captain, being greatly pleased with his shave, said to him: "You are welcome to bring your comrade every night and sup with me."

The barber went back to the dyer with all the food he had earned and found Abu Kir asleep. So he woke him. When the dyer opened his eyes and saw the food, he said, "Where did you get all this?"

"From Allah," Abu Sir said. "But do not eat this, O my brother. Leave it to serve us another time. For know that I shaved the captain, and I mentioned to him our lack of food. Upon this he said, 'Welcome to you! Bring your comrade and sup with me every night'."

But Abu Kir replied: "My head is going around with seasickness and I cannot rise from my place. So let me sup off these things and you go alone to the captain."

"There is no harm in that," Abu Sir replied. And he sat looking at the other as he ate, gulping down food with the gulp of an elephant who has not eaten for days. He bit off a mouthful before he had swallowed down the last one and made noises like a hungry bull puffing over his beans and crushed straw.

Then up came a sailor and said to Abu Sir, "The captain asks you and your comrade to come to supper."

"Will you come with us?" Abu Sir asked the dyer.

But he said, "I cannot walk."

So the barber went by himself and found the captain sitting in front of a great tray. On it were twenty or more dishes.

"Where is your friend?" the captain asked Abu Sir.

"O my lord, he is seasick," the barber answered.

"That won't do him any harm," the captain said. "His sickness will soon pass off. But you take his supper to him and come back." And he took some of each dish and put it into a bowl, enough for ten, saying, "Take this to your friend."

So the barber carried the bowl to the dyer and found him busily grinding away at the food which was before him.

"Didn't I say to you, 'Don't eat this'?" said Abu Sir. "Indeed the captain is a kindly man. See what he has sent you because I told him you were seasick."

"Give it here," cried the dyer.

So the barber gave him the bowl, and Abu Kir snatched it from him and fell on the food like a raging lion or a man nearly dead from hunger.

Abu Sir left him and went back. He supped and enjoyed himself and drank coffee with the captain. After this he returned to Abu Kir and found that he had eaten all that was in the bowl and had thrown it aside empty. So he picked it up and gave it to one of the captain's servants. Then he went back to Abu Kir and slept.

Next day he continued to shave the passengers, and everything he got by way of meat and drink he gave to his shipmate, who ate and drank and sat still. And every evening Abu Sir brought Abu Kir a full bowl from the captain's table besides. Thus they continued day by day for twenty days.

3. The Good Fortune of Abu Kir

When the ship came into the harbor of a city, the dyer and the barber landed. They hired a room at an inn. The barber bought a cooking pot and a platter and spoons and brought food and cooked it. But Abu Kir fell asleep the moment they got to the inn. Nor did he wake up till Abu Sir set the tray of food before him.

"Do not blame me," said the dyer when he had eaten. "For I am still giddy." And he fell asleep again.

Thus he did for forty days while every day the barber went about the city plying his trade. Always when he returned, he found the dyer asleep and aroused him. The moment he woke, Abu Kir fell on the food, eating like one who can never get his fill or be satisfied. After this he went to sleep again.

"Sit up and be comfortable, or go out and walk about the city," Abu Sir would say to him. "It is a gay place. There is not its equal among the cities."

But the dyer would always reply, "Do not blame me, for I am giddy."

Abu Sir didn't want to hurt his feelings or give him hard words. But on the forty-first day the barber himself felt sick and could not go out. Abu Kir would still do nothing but eat and sleep, while each day Abu Sir got worse. After four days the dyer, feeling the sharp pangs of hunger, got up.

He looked in the barber's clothes. There he found a thousand silver pieces. He took them and went out without a word to anyone.

Going to the bazaar, Abu Kir bought himself some costly clothes. Then he went strolling about the city. And as he strolled, he noted a strange thing: All the people were dressed in clothes of white and blue and no other color. And when he came to a dyer's shop, there too he saw nothing but blue.

Abu Kir pulled out a kerchief and said to the dyer, "O master, take this and dye it red."

"I will dye it blue," the man said.

"But I want it dyed red."

"I don't know how to dye it red."

"Then dye it green."

"I don't know how to dye it green."

No matter what tint Abu Kir named, the man could not dye it that color. And he said to Abu Kir, "There are forty master dyers in this city, and not one knows how to dye any color but blue."

Then Abu Kir said: "Know that I, too, am a dyer. And I know how to dye all colors. Take me into your service and I will teach you all my art."

But the other said, "We never admit a stranger into our craft. It's against our rules."

"And what if I open a dye shop myself?"

"We will not let you do that."

At this Abu Kir went out and offered his services to another dyer. He got the same answer from him. And when he had made the round of all forty dyers and got the same answer from them all, he became angry. He went to the King of the city and complained to him.

"O King of the Age," he said, "I am a stranger and a dyer by trade." Then he told the King what had passed between himself and the dyers of the town.

"I can dye any color," he added. "I can dye various kinds of red, such as rose color and plum color; and various kinds of green, such as grass-green, and olive, and parrot's wing; and various shades of yellow, such as orange and lemon color." And he went on to name the rest of the colors.

Then he said: "O King of the Age, all the dyers in your city cannot turn out one of these colors. They don't know how to dye any color but blue. Yet they will not admit me among them, either as master or workman."

"I will open a dye shop for you," the King said, "and give you capital. And have no concern about the dyers. If one of them tries to stop you, I will hang him over his shop door."

Then the King sent for builders and said to them: "Go round about the city with this master dyer. What-ever place pleases him, turn out the owner and build him a dye shop after his wish. Whatever he tells you to do, do it."

The King also gave Abu Kir fine clothes and a furnished house and slaves and servants and money and a horse to ride on. Abu Kir put on the fine clothes, mounted the horse, and rode through the city. The architects went before him. The dyer looked about him till he saw a place which pleased him. Then he said, "This is a good place." At this the architects turned the owner out and took him to the King, who gave the man what contented him and more. Then the builders fell to work.

"Build thus and thus and do this and that," Abu Kir said to them.

So they built him a dye shop that did not have its equal. When it was done, Abu Kir went to the King and told him that now all he needed was the price of the dye and materials to set things going.

"Take these four thousand dinars," the King said, "and let me see the first fruits of your work." And he sent Abu Kir five hundred pieces of stuff to dye.

Abu Kir took the money and bought dye and all the materials he needed for dyeing. He taught ten of his slaves the whole craft of dyeing. He himself didn't have to put his hand to anything. He sat among his cushions like a mighty lord, only saying to the slaves, "Do this and do that!"

Abu Kir dyed the five hundred pieces of cloth the King had sent him and hung them up to dry. And when the people passed by the shop, they saw a wonder-sight such as they had never in their lives seen. They crowded about the entrance.

"O master, what are the names of these colors?" they asked.

Abu Kir said, "This is red and that yellow and the other green." And he named all the colors.

So people began to bring him cloth to dye, saying, "Dye it for us like this and that, and take what pay you will for your labor."

When Abu Kir had made an end of dyeing the King's stuffs, he took them and went with them to the audience chamber. The King was delighted and gave Abu Kir much money. All the troops also brought him stuffs. He dyed them any color they wished, and they threw him gold and silver. His fame spread. Good came in to him at every door. And none of the other dyers could say a word to him.

They used to come kissing his hands and excusing themselves for having mistreated him.

"Let us work for you," they said.

But he would have none of them, for he had slaves and great wealth.

4. The Comrades Meet Again

This is how things went with Abu Kir. Now as regards Abu Sir.

After Abu Kir had stolen his money, Abu Sir lay senseless for three days. Then the porter at the inn said to himself: I have not seen or heard anything of the two companions in a long time. Perhaps they have made off without paying. Perhaps they are dead or something.

He waited till sunset, then went up to the door of their room. Abu Sir was groaning inside. Hearing this, the porter went in.

"No harm to you," he said. "Where is your friend?"

"By Allah, I don't know," Abu Sir replied. "I came to my senses only today. I called out, but no one answered my call. O my brother, look for the purse in the garments under my head, and go buy me something to eat, for I am very hungry."

The porter looked and found the purse.

"This purse is empty," he said. "There is nothing in it."

Then Abu Sir knew that Abu Kir had taken his money and fled.

"Have you seen my friend?" he asked of the porter.

"I have not seen him for three days," the porter answered. "Indeed, I thought the two of you had gone away."

"Not so!" the barber cried. "But he took my money and fled, seeing me sick."

Then Abu Sir began to weep and wail. But the porter, seeing how matters stood, said, "No harm shall befall you, and Allah will pay him back for his deed." Then he went away and cooked some broth and brought it to Abu Sir. And he tended the barber for two months, spending his own money on Abu Sir.

At last the barber was well of his sickness. He stood up and went out and walked about the market streets.

In front of one fine shop, Abu Sir saw dyed stuffs spread out and a crowd of people looking at them. So he questioned one of the townsmen, saying: "What place is this? And why are the people crowding together so?"

"This is the King's Dye Shop," the man said, "which he set up for a foreigner called Abu Kir. Whenever he dyes new stuff, we all flock to him and amuse ourselves by gazing on his work. For we have no dyers in our land who know how to dye these colors." And he went on to tell the barber all that had happened between Abu Kir and the dyers, and how the King had built him the dye shop and given him this and that. In brief, he told him all that had occurred.

At this the barber rejoiced. He said to himself:
Praised be Allah who has made my comrade prosper! He
has forgotten me only because he is so busy. It is
excusable. But I acted kindly by him when he was out
of work. So when he sees me, he will rejoice and do by
me as I did by him.

He pushed his way through the crowd and made for
the door of the dye shop.

Abu Kir was sitting on cushions spread on a bench
beside the doorway. He was clad in royal garments, and
four white slaves and four black slaves waited on him.

The barber went up and stood before him, smiling with pleasure, bowing, and expecting to be made much of. But when Abu Kir's eye met the barber's eye, the dyer cried: "O scoundrel, how many times have I bidden you not to stand at the door of the workshop? Do you have a mind to disgrace me with the people, thief that you are? Seize him!"

At this the slaves laid hold of Abu Sir. And the dyer rose up from his seat and said, "Throw him down!"

So they threw him down, and Abu Kir took a stick and dealt him a hundred strokes on the back. After this they turned him over and he beat him a hundred strokes on the belly.

Then the dyer said: "O villain, if ever again I see you standing at the door of this dye shop, I will send you to the King. He will have your head cut off. Begone!" So Abu Sir went away broken-hearted because of the beating and the shame that had fallen on him. And the bystanders asked Abu Kir, "What has this man done?"

"The fellow is a thief who steals the people's stuffs," Abu Kir told them. "He has robbed me many a time. And I kept saying to myself, 'Allah forgive him, for he is a poor man.' I didn't want to deal roughly with him. So I used to pay my customers for the cloth he had stolen. But he would not stop stealing. If ever he comes here again, I will send him to the King, who will put him to death and rid the people of his mischief."

5. The Baths

Such was the behavior of Abu Kir. But as regards Abu Sir, he went back to the inn and sat thinking about how the dyer had treated him, returning evil for good. And he sat there till the burning of the beating was somewhat less. Then he decided to go to the Baths, the Hammam, to soothe his pain.

So he went out and walked about the market streets. And he asked one of the townspeople, "O my brother, which is the way to the Baths?"

Said the man, "And what manner of thing may the Baths be?"

"It's a place where people wash themselves and do away with their dirt," the barber said. "And it is one of the best of the good things in the world."

"Go to the sea," the townsman said.

But the barber said, "I want the Baths."

"We don't know what manner of thing the Baths are," said the other. "We all go to the sea. Even the King goes to the sea to wash himself."

When Abu Sir understood there were no Baths in the city and that the people had never heard of them, he went to the palace. He fell on his face before the King, kissed the ground between his hands, and called down blessings on him. Then he said: "O King of the Age, I am a stranger and a bathman by trade. I entered your city and thought to go to the Baths. But I found not one here. How comes a city so fine as this to be without the Baths?"

"What manner of thing is the Baths?" asked the King. "I have not heard of it."

So Abu Sir told him and said, "Your capital will not be a perfect city till there be a Baths in it."

"Welcome to you!" said the King. And he clad the barber in fine clothes and gave him a horse and slaves and a furnished house. And he honored him even more than he had honored the dyer.

After this he summoned builders and said to them, "Go to Abu Sir and build him Baths in whatever place pleases him."

Abu Sir took them and walked with them through the city till they saw a place that pleased him. He pointed it out to the builders and they set to work and built him Baths that had no equal. Then he had them paint the Hammam so that it was a delight to see. After this Abu Sir went to the King and told him that they had finished building and decorating the Baths.

"Now nothing is lacking but the furniture," he said.

The King gave him ten thousand dinars. With this Abu Sir furnished the Baths. And when he had hung the towels on the ropes, all who passed by the door stared.

They crowded around and said, "What is this thing?"

To which Abu Sir replied, "This is the Hammam. This is the Baths."

They marveled at it. Then Abu Sir heated water and set the bath a-working. The people lost their wits over the jetting fountain that spouted into the great basin. And he sought out ten clever slave boys and taught them how to shampoo.

"Do like this with the bathers," he said.

Then he burned perfumes and sent out a crier to cry aloud in the city, saying, "O creatures of Allah, get you to the Baths which are called the King's Hammam!"

So the best of the people came and Abu Sir bade the slave boys wash their bodies. The people went down into the tank, and coming out, they sat on a raised pavement. And the boys shampooed them as they had been taught by Abu Sir. And for three days he took no pay from anyone.

On the fourth day the barber invited the King, who forthwith mounted his horse and rode to the Baths with his ministers. Abu Sir himself helped the King take off his clothes and soaped his body and rubbed it with the bag-gloves. After this thorough washing, Abu Sir mingled rosewater with the water in the tank, and the King went into it. And when he came out from the tank, the King felt a lightness such as he had never known in all of his life.

Then the barber made him sit on the dais, and the slave boys shampooed him while the odor of burning perfumes rose around.

And the King said to the barber, "O master, is this the Hammam?"

And Abu Sir said, "Yes."

Then the King said, "As I live, my city was not a city till it had this Bath."

When the Queen heard from her lord what a pleasure the Hammam was, she desired to go there, too. So on her account Abu Sir divided the day into two parts. Between dawn and noon, the Hammam was for men. Between midday and sundown, it was for women. And he taught four slave girls the service of the Hammam so they became expert bathwomen.

When the Queen entered, Abu Sir stationed a handmaid behind the pay chest. Into this the Queen put a thousand dinars, she was so pleased. And everybody in the city heard about it, and the fame of the Baths increased.

Good came in to Abu Sir at every door. He got acquainted with the royal guards and had many close friends among them. The King himself used to come to him one day every week and always left him a thousand dinars. The other days were for rich and poor alike. And all were equally pleased, for Abu Sir dealt courteously with all the folk and treated everybody with respect.

6. Abu Kir Makes a Suggestion

Thus it went with Abu Sir. Now as regards Abu Kir. The dyer heard the people praising the Baths and saying: "In truth this Hammam is the Paradise of this world. You must go with us tomorrow to this delightful Bath."

Abu Kir said to himself, I must go like the rest of the world. I must see this Bath that has taken the people's wits from them.

So he put on his richest clothes and mounted his horse and rode to the Hammam. Eight slaves attended him, four walking in front and four behind.

When he got down at the door, he smelt the odor of burning aloes wood. People were going in and out. And the benches were full of rich and poor.

When he saw Abu Kir come in, Abu Sir rose and greeted him with joy. But the dyer said to him: "Is this the way for well-bred men to behave? I have opened a dye shop and am a great man in this city. I know the King. Yet you did not ask about me. You did not say, 'Where is my comrade?' As for me, I looked for you in vain. I sent my slaves to search for you in all the inns and other places. But they did not know where you had gone. Nor could anyone give me news of you."

Abu Sir said: "What? Did I not come to you? And did you not call me a thief and beat me and dishonor me before the world?"

"What kind of talk is this?" said the dyer. "Was it you whom I beat?"

"Yes, it was I."

At this Abu Kir swore a thousand oaths that he had not recognized Abu Sir.

"There was a fellow like you," he said, "who used to steal my cloth, and I took you for him." And he went on to pretend he was so sorry, and struck his hands together, and raised his eyes to heaven. "Indeed we have sinned against you," he said. "But why did you not tell me who you were? Indeed the fault is yours because you did not make yourself known to me."

And Abu Sir replied: "Allah pardon you, O my comrade. Enter and take off your clothes and bathe at your ease."

Said the dyer, "I beg you, by Allah, O my brother, forgive me!"

And Abu Sir said, "Allah take your blame away and forgive you!"

Then Abu Kir asked, "Where did you get all this?"

"He who made you prosper," Abu Sir replied, "made me prosper, too. I went to the King and told him all about the Hammam, and he bade me build one."

The dyer said: "I know the King well. I will make

him love and favor you more than ever for my sake. He does not know that you are my comrade, but I will tell him. I will speak kindly of you to him."

"There is no need to do that," Abu Sir said. "The King and all his court love me and have given me this and that. But now, take off your clothes behind the chest and enter the Hammam, and I will go in with you and rub you down with the gloves."

So Abu Kir took off his clothes and Abu Sir entered the bath with him and soaped him and gloved him. And when Abu Kir came out and dressed himself, Abu Sir brought him dinner and sherbets. All the people marveled at the honor Abu Sir did him. The dyer wanted to pay him, but Abu Sir would not accept anything from his old friend.

"Shame on such doing!" he said. "You are my comrade."

Then the dyer said: "By Allah, O my comrade, this is a mighty fine Hammam you have here. But there is one thing missing."

"And what is that?" asked Abu Sir.

"You do not have the paste which removes hair from the body with comfort. Prepare it. And the next time the King comes, give it to him and he will love you with great love and honor."

"You are right," said Abu Sir. "I will make it at once. I forgot all about it."

Abu Kir went out of the Baths, mounted his horse, and went straight to the King.

"I have a warning to give you, O King of the Age," the dyer said.

"What is your warning?" asked the King.

"I hear that you have built a Hammam."

"Yes," said the King. "A stranger came to me and I built the Baths for him even as I built a dye shop for you. And, indeed, it is a mighty fine Hammam and an ornament to my city."

"Have you gone there to bathe?" asked the dyer.

"Yes," said the King.

Then Abu Kir cried out, "Praised be God who saved you from the mischief of that villain the bathkeeper!"

"And what of him?" the King inquired.

"Know, O King of the Age," said the dyer, "that if you enter the Hammam again, you will surely perish."

"How so?"

And the dyer said: "This bathkeeper is your foe. He got you to build this Bath because he means to poison you. He has made something for you. When you enter the Hammam, he will offer it to you, saying, 'This is a drug which will remove hair from the body with comfort.' Now, it is no drug but a deadly poison."

When the King heard this, he said, "Keep this secret." And to himself he said, I will visit the Hammam and see if this be true.

7. Abu Sir in Trouble

So next day the King went to the Baths.

Abu Sir began to bathe him, and as he did so he said, "O King of the Age, I have made a paste which helps to take the lower hair off the body."

"Bring it to me," said the King.

So the barber brought it. When the King smelled the paste and found it to have a disagreeable odor, he was sure it was a poison. And he called out to his guards, "Seize him!"

So they seized Abu Sir. Then the King put on his clothes and, boiling with fury, went to his audience chamber. There he had Abu Sir brought before him with his elbows tied behind him. And the King sent for his sea captain and said to him, "Take this villain and set him in a sack with quicklime in it. Then put him in a boat and row out with him in front of my palace. I will be sitting at the lattice. Then ask me, 'Shall I cast him in?' And if I answer, 'Cast him!' throw the sack into the sea so he shall die drowned and burned."

"I hear and obey," said the captain. And he took Abu Sir to an island facing the King's palace.

But when they got to the island, the captain said to the barber: "Ho you! Once I visited your Hammam.

You treated me with honor, doing everything for me yourself. I had great comfort from your Baths. Moreover, you refused to take any pay from me, and I love you with great love. So tell me, what have you done that the king wants you to die?"

"I have done nothing," Abu Sir said. "Nor do I know of any wrong I have done against him which deserves this."

Then the captain said. "You were very high in the King's favor, and all prosperous men are envied. Perhaps someone was jealous of your good fortune and told the King something that angered him against you. But be of good cheer. No harm shall befall you. For even as you treated me, so will I treat you. However, if I set you free, you must stay with me on this island till some ship sails from our city to your native land. Then I will send you there."

Abu Sir kissed his hand and thanked him. After this the captain brought the quicklime. He put it in a sack together with a great stone the size of a man.

"I put my trust in Allah!" he said. "I will go now and pretend to cast you in the sea. In the meantime you take this net and cast it in the sea and perhaps you will catch some fish. For I am bound to supply the King's kitchen with fish every day, but today I was busy with what has befallen you. I fear that the cook's men may come for fish and find none."

"Go, and God help you!" said Abu Sir. "And I will fish the while."

So the captain set the sack in the boat and paddled it till it came under the palace. And when he saw the King seated at the lattice, he said to him, "O King of the Age, shall I cast him in?"

"Cast him!" cried the King and waved his hand. And lo and behold! something flashed like lightning and fell in the sea.

Now that which had fallen into the water was the King's seal ring. It was an enchanted ring, and this was the manner of its power. When the King was angry with anyone and wanted to slay him, he had but to sign to him with his right hand. At once lightning would flash from the ring and kill that person. The King's troops knew this and feared the ring. They obeyed him because of the ring. And he overcame men of might only by means of the ring.

So when it fell from his finger, the King hid the matter and kept silence. He dared not say, "My ring has fallen into the sea." He feared that if this were known, his troops would rise up and slay him.

8. The King's Signet Ring

This is what befell the King. But as regards Abu Sir, he was casting his net into the sea. In a little while he drew it up full of fish. Then he cast again, and after that again, till he had a great mound of fish before him. And he said to himself: "By Allah, it is a long time since I ate fish. When the captain returns, I will ask him to broil a fish for me so I may dine on it."

He chose a large, fat fish for himself and with his knife cut the fish's throat. Then he slit open its belly to clean it. And lo! when he looked, he found the King's signet ring in the belly. For the fish had swallowed the ring, and Fate had driven the fish to the island.

Abu Sir took the ring and put it on the little finger of his right hand. And soon after this the cook's men came up for fish.

"O man," they said to Abu Sir, "where is the captain gone?"

"I know not," said Abu Sir, waving his right hand.

There was a sudden flash, and the two men fell down dead.

Abu Sir stood in amaze. He did not know what had killed them and he was full of grief. He was still pondering it when the captain suddenly returned. He

saw the mound of fishes and the two men lying dead and the seal ring on Abu Sir's finger. And he said, "O my brother, do not move the hand on which you have the signet ring! Else it will kill me!"

Abu Sir wondered at this speech, but he kept his hand still. Then the captain pointed to the bodies and said, "Who slew these two men?"

"By Allah, my brother," said Abu Sir, "I know not."

Then the captain said, "Tell me where you got the ring that is on your finger."

"I found it in this fish's belly," replied Abu Sir.

"You speak the truth," the captain said, "for I saw the ring fall flashing from the King's palace and disappear in the sea. When the King said, 'Cast him!' the ring slipped from his finger and fell into the sea. There the fish swallowed it, and Allah drove the fish to you, for it was your fate to get the ring. But do you know its power?"

And Abu Sir said, "I did not know that it had any special power."

"Learn, then," said the captain, "that the King's troops obey him only out of fear of this signet ring. There is a spell on it. When anyone has a mind to kill the King, the King will sign at him with the ring, and that man's head will drop from between his shoulders. A flash of lightning comes from the ring and the ray strikes the object of his anger."

When he heard this, Abu Sir cried out with joy. "Take me back to the city!" he implored.

"That I will," replied the captain, "now that I no longer fear that the King will do you harm."

So saying, he took Abu Sir back in a boat, and Abu Sir landed and went to the palace. He found the King sitting with his ministers in the council chamber. His face was full of trouble and care about the ring, but still he dared not tell anyone he had lost it.

When he set eyes on Abu Sir, the King cried out in amaze: "Did we not cast you into the sea? How then did you come out?"

Abu Sir replied, "O King of the Age, when you bade the captain throw me into the sea, he carried me to an island and asked me why you were angered at me. 'What have you done,' he asked me, 'that the King should want you to die this foul death?' I answered, 'By Allah, I do not know. I have done him no wrong.' He said: 'You were high in the King's favor. Perhaps someone envied you and threw out certain hints about you to him so that he got angry with you. But when I visited your Hammam, you treated me with honor, and I will do by you as you did by me.'

"Then he set a great stone in the sack instead of me and cast it into the sea. But when you signed to him to cast me in, your seal ring dropped from your finger into the sea and a fish swallowed it. Now I was on the island a-fishing, and this fish came up in the net with others. I took it intending to broil it. When I opened its belly, I found the signet ring. So I took it and put it on my finger.

"Then up came two servants of the kitchen, looking for fish. I did not know the power of the ring and signed to them with my hand. At once they fell dead. Then the captain came back, and seeing the ring on my finger, told me its spell. And behold, I have brought it back to you, for you dealt kindly with me, and your kindness is not lost upon me. Here is your ring. Take it! But if I have done anything to you that deserves death, tell me my crime and slay me."

So saying, he pulled the ring from his finger and gave it to the King.

Then the King saw that Abu Kir had lied to him about Abu Sir. He saw now that Abu Sir had never intended to poison him. Since the barber knew the power of the ring, he could have slain him had he wished to do so. But he had brought the ring back to him instead.

Rising to his feet the King embraced Abu Sir.

"Forgive me the wrong I have done you," he said. "If anyone but you had got hold of this ring, he would never have restored it to me."

"O King of the Age," Abu Sir said, "if you would have me forgive you, tell me what was my fault that drew your anger upon me."

"By Allah," answered the King, "it is clear to me that you are not guilty of anything. Only the dyer told me such and such things about you." And he told Abu Sir how the dyer had come to warn him about the poison which was no poison. Abu Sir in his turn told the King the story of his friendship with Abu Kir, from first to last.

"He was my comrade and neighbor in Alexandria," Abu Sir said. "We went out to seek our fortunes together. We were to be like brothers. He who got work was to feed him who was out of work. We recited the Opening Chapter of the Koran together to seal our bond." And he went on to tell the King all that had happened between them.

Then he added: "O King of the Age, it was he who counseled me to make the paste. 'Your Hammam is perfect,' he said. 'It lacks only the paste that removes hair with comfort.' This paste is harmless, and we use it in our land as part of the service of the Hammam — I had forgotten about it. But now send for the workmen of the dye shop. Question them all about what I have told you."

The King sent for them and questioned them one and all, and they showed him the truth of the matter. Then the King commanded his guards to bring the dyer before him, saying, "Bring him barefooted, bareheaded, and with his elbows tied."

9. The Goodness of Abu Sir

So they brought Abu Kir bound before the King. The dyer saw Abu Sir seated by the King's side. And the porter of the inn and the workmen of the shop were standing before him.

The porter said to him, "Is not this your comrade whom you robbed and left sick in the room?"

And the workmen said to him, "Is not this the man you bade us seize and beat?"

So Abu Kir's wickedness was made clear to the King. And he said to his guards: "Take him and parade him about the city and the markets. Then set him in a sack with quicklime and cast him into the sea that he may be drowned and burned."

At this Abu Sir cried out, "O King of the Age, forgive him, for I pardon him for all he has done to me."

But the King said, "Although you pardon him for all he has done to you, I cannot pardon him for all he has done to me." And he called out to his guards, "Take him!"

Then the King said to the barber, who stood with his head bowed and his face full of sorrow, "O Abu Sir, ask what you will of me and it shall be given you."

And Abu Sir answered, "I ask of you to send me back to my own country, for I do not care to stay here any longer."

The King offered to make Abu Sir his Wazir, his prime minister. But Abu Sir would not accept.

Then the King bestowed great gifts on the barber, greater and more than he had already given him. And amongst the rest was a ship full of goods and a crew of slaves. So Abu Sir said farewell to the King and sailed home in his own ship, manned by his own crew. Nor did he cast anchor till he reached Alexandria and made fast to the shore.

Now as he was landing, one of his crew came running to him and said, "O my lord, there is a great heavy sack on the seashore. The mouth of the sack is tied, and I do not know what is in there."

So Abu Sir went up to look. Opening the sack he found in it the body of Abu Kir, which the sea had carried there.

The barber took the body of the dyer and buried it near Alexandria. Over the grave he built a tomb. And near the tomb of Abu Kir, he built his own tomb. For in spite of everything, Abu Sir wished to lie beside his comrade when Allah should take him to himself.